BAGDASARIAN
P R O D U C T I O N S

ALVINNN!!!
AND THE CHIPMUNKS™
The Fun Dad

based on the screenplay "Who's Your Daddy?"
written by Janice Karman
adapted by Lauren Forte

Ready-to-Read

Simon Spotlight
New York   London   Toronto   Sydney   New Delhi

SIMON SPOTLIGHT
An imprint of Simon & Schuster Children's Publishing Division
1230 Avenue of the Americas, New York, New York 10020
This Simon Spotlight edition October 2018
For information about special discounts for bulk purchases, please contact
Simon & Schuster Special Sales at 1-866-506-1949 or business@simonandschuster.com.
Manufactured in the United States of America 0818 LAK
10 9 8 7 6 5 4 3 2 1
ISBN 978-1-5344-2445-6 (hc)
ISBN 978-1-5344-2444-9 (pbk)
ISBN 978-1-5344-2446-3 (eBook)

Dave was not feeling well.
"Achoo!" He sneezed as he drove
Theodore to his play rehearsal.

"'Mr. Humble, so kind of you to stop by,'" said a girl practicing her line. "'Why, thank you, dear. I hope . . .'" Theo paused. "Dave, you're supposed to cue me!" he continued.

But Dave was fast asleep.

The doctor told Dave to stay in bed.
"Don't worry," Alvin whispered as
Dave fell asleep. "I'll take over
dad duty."

"Well, boys," Alvin said.
"Looks like I'm your new dad!"

"I'm not letting you parent us," Simon insisted. "It is really hard. You'll be terrible at it."

"I'd be a great dad! Let's bet," Alvin argued.

"Okay. If you're not a good parent," said Simon, "we take a meditation class."

"Fine. But if I'm good," Alvin said, "you take karate with *me*."

The next morning, Theodore and Simon were hungry. "What's for breakfast, *Dad*?" Simon asked sarcastically.

"Glad you asked," Alvin answered.
"A balanced meal of pie and popcorn!"
Simon shook his head.
But Theo loved it!

After breakfast Alvin took
the boys to school.
"This is humiliating!" Simon cried.

Later that night Alvin made dinner.
It was a little burnt.

Then he tried to clean up.
He overloaded the
garbage disposal.

Theo asked for help rehearsing his play lines.
Alvin made paint balloons instead.

"What kind of dad are you?"
said Simon.
"I'm the fun dad!" Alvin said,
tossing a balloon at him.

"Alvin, I need a costume
for my play," Theo said.
"Wouldn't you rather play
than be *in* a play?" Alvin asked.
"Not really," Theo answered.
"You should quit," Alvin said.

"You took him out of the play?"
Simon said angrily. "A good parent
isn't selfish. You lost our bet."
"You're not the judge," Alvin said.

Simon sat in a meditation pose and said, "Okay. Let's get a group together to judge. You choose three and I'll choose three."

The Chipettes and three bullies from school came over. "Members of the board," Simon called, "after hearing all the evidence, please raise a hand if you think Alvin is a good parent." No one moved.

"What?!" shouted Alvin.
"I handpicked you guys!"
"Well, you're a terrible parent,"
said Derek the bully.

"Simon, please give me another
chance," Alvin begged.
"I don't want to lose the bet,
but I also want to prove
I can do this."

Simon gave him a second chance.
That day Alvin went food shopping
and made a great dinner.

Then he got Theodore back in the play and started making his costume.

Soon Dave was feeling well again.
He walked into the living room
and was shocked!
"What happened here?"

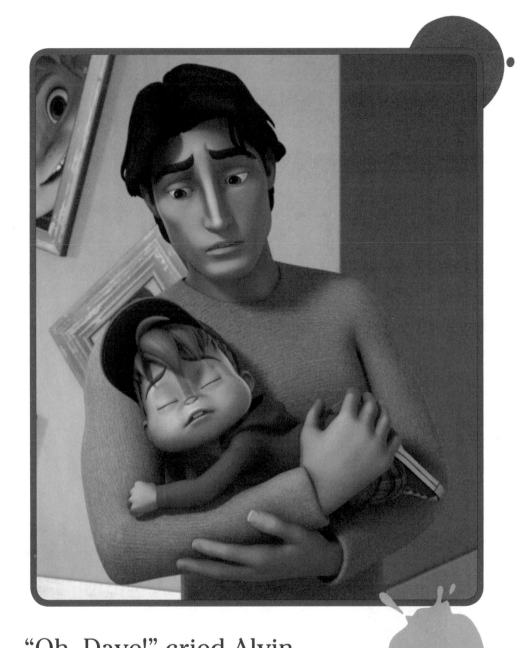

"Oh, Dave!" cried Alvin.
"I thought I could do it,
but parenting is hard.
I don't want to do it anymore!"
"Don't worry," Dave said. "I'll help."

Together, they cleaned
and scrubbed and straightened
up the house.

When Simon and Theodore got home,
Alvin lay exhausted on the floor.
"You did it!" said Simon. "You win!"
"Well, thank you, Simon. I accept
your defeat," Alvin replied.

Dave entered the room.

"Good news! I fixed the leak!"

"I guess I *did* have help," Alvin said.

"Dave, Alvin is going to need a yoga mat!" Simon said.

The next day Simon was meditating in yoga class. "Ommmm," he chanted.

Alvin sat right next to him.
"Ommmm—my gosh, this
stiiiinks!" he muttered
under his breath.